NURSERY
Songs & Lullabies

featuring the art of
BESSIE PEASE GUTMANN

GROSSET & DUNLAP

Song Titles in Alphabetical Order

OVER IN THE MEADOW

Brightly

Traditional

O - ver in the mead - ow, in the sand, in the sun, Lived an

old — moth - er frog — and her lit - tle frog - gie one.

"Croak!" said the moth - er; "I croak," said the one, So they

croaked and were hap - py in the sand, in the sun.

Over in the meadow, in the pond so blue,
Lived an old mother fish and her little fishies two.
"Swim!" said the mother; "We swim," said the two,
So they swam and were happy in the pond so blue.

Over in the meadow, in the nest in the tree,
Lived an old mother bird and her little birdies three.
"Sing!" said the mother; "We sing," said the three,
So they sang and were happy in the nest in the tree.

ALL THROUGH THE NIGHT

Slowly

Old Welsh Air

Sleep, my child, and peace at-tend thee, All through the night; Guard-ian an-gels God will send thee, All through the night; Soft the drow-sy hours are creep-ing, Hill and vale in slum-ber sleep-ing, — I my lov-ing vig-il keep-ing, All through the night.

While the moon her watch is keeping,
All through the night;
While the weary world is sleeping,
All through the night;
O'er thy spirit gently stealing,
Visions of delight revealing,
Breathes a pure and holy feeling,
All through the night.

ROCK-A-BYE, BABY

Traditional

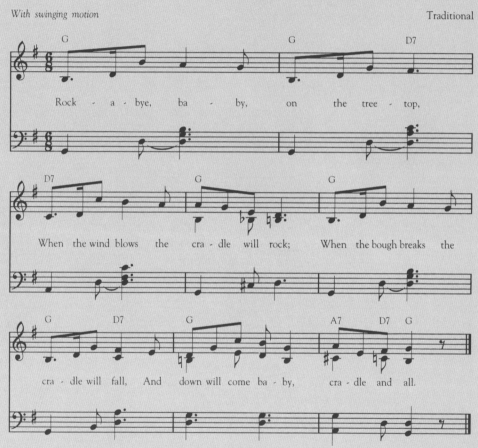

Rock - a - bye, ba - by, on the tree - top,

When the wind blows the cra - dle will rock; When the bough breaks the

cra - dle will fall, And down will come ba - by, cra - dle and all.

TWINKLE, TWINKLE, LITTLE STAR

Sweetly

Traditional

When the blazing sun is gone,
When he nothing shines upon,
Then you show your little light,
Twinkle, twinkle all the night.
Twinkle, twinkle, little star,
How I wonder what you are!

Then the traveler in the dark
Thanks you for your tiny spark;
He could not see which way to go,
If you did not twinkle so.
Twinkle, twinkle, little star,
How I wonder what you are!

HUSH, LITTLE BABY

Gently

A Southern Lullaby

Hush, lit - tle ba - by, don't say a word,

Ma - ma's going to buy you a mock - ing - bird. 2. And if that mock - ing -

bird don't sing, Ma - ma's going to buy you a dia - mond ring. 3. And

3. . . . if that diamond ring turns brass,
Mama's going to buy you a looking glass.

4. And if that looking glass gets broke,
Mama's going to buy you a billy goat.

5. And if that billy goat won't pull,
Mama's going to buy you a cart and bull.

6. And if that cart and bull turn over,
Mama's going to buy you a dog named Rover.

7. And if that dog named Rover won't bark,
Mama's going to buy you a horse and cart.

8. And if that horse and cart fall down,
You'll still be the sweetest little baby in town.

WHERE IS THUMBKIN?

Spirited

Traditional Finger Play

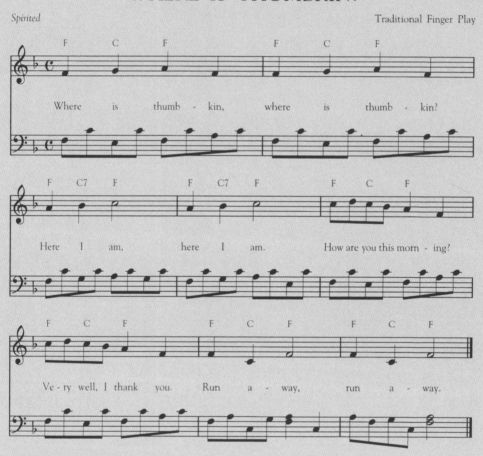

Where is thumb - kin, where is thumb - kin?

Here I am, here I am. How are you this morn - ing?

Ve - ry well, I thank you. Run a - way, run a - way.

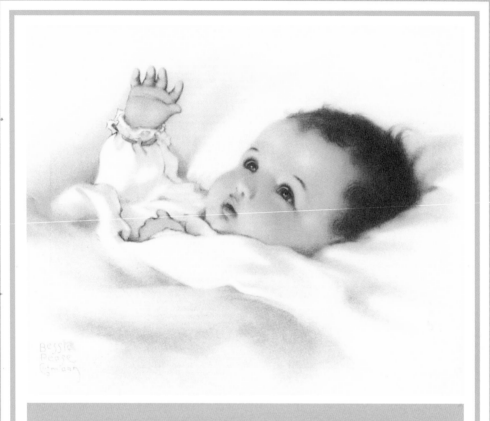

Where is pointer, etc.
Where is tall man, etc.
Where is ring man, etc.
Where is pinkie, etc.
Where's the whole family, etc.

HEY DIDDLE DIDDLE

Lively   Traditional

Hey did - dle did - dle, The cat and the fid - dle, The
cow jumped o - ver the moon, _____ The lit - tle dog laughed to
see such sport, And the dish ran a - way with the spoon. _____

LULLABY AND GOOD NIGHT

Tenderly   Johannes Brahms

Lul - la - by and good night, with _ ro - ses be - dight, _ With _

lil - ies be - decked, is _ ba - by's wee bed. Lay thee

down now and rest, may thy slum - ber be blest, Lay thee

down now and rest, may thy slum - ber be blest.

Lullaby and good night,
Thy mother's delight,
Bright angels around
My darling shall stand.
They will guard thee from harms,
Thou shalt wake in my arms,
They will guard thee from harms,
Thou shalt wake in my arms.

THE ANIMAL FAIR

Brightly   Minstrel Song

I went to the a-ni-mal fair, _____ The birds and the beasts were there, _____ The big ba-boon by the light of the moon Was comb-ing his au-burn hair, _____ The mon-key bumped the skunk, _____ And sat on the e-le-phant's trunk; _____ The e-le-phant sneezed and fell to his knees, And that was the end of the monk, the monk, the monk, the monk, the monk. The monk. The monk.

THE MULBERRY BUSH

Happily

Traditional

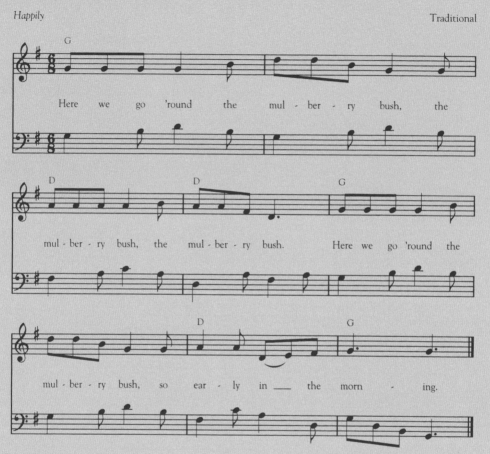

Here we go 'round the mul-ber-ry bush, the mul-ber-ry bush, the mul-ber-ry bush. Here we go 'round the mul-ber-ry bush, so ear-ly in ___ the morn - ing.

This is the way we wash our clothes, etc.,
So early Monday morning.

This is the way we iron our clothes, etc.,
So early Tuesday morning.

This is the way we mend our clothes, etc.,
So early Wednesday morning.

This is the way we sweep the floor, etc.,
So early Thursday morning.

This is the way we scrub the floor, etc.,
So early Friday morning.

This is the way we bake our bread, etc.,
So early Saturday morning.

This is the way we go to church, etc.,
So early Sunday morning.

ALPHABET SONG

ABCDEFGHIJK
LMNOPQRST
UVWXYZ

NOW THE DAY IS OVER

Leisurely

Joseph Barnby

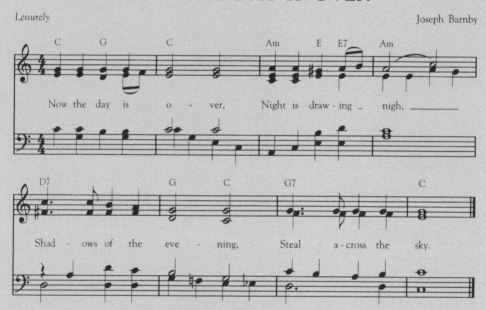

Now the day is o - ver, Night is draw - ing _ nigh, _____

Shad - ows of the eve - ning, Steal a - cross the sky.

Now the darkness gathers,
Stars begin to peep,
Birds and beasts and flowers
Soon will be asleep.

FATHER, WE THANK THEE

Thankfully

Traditional Prayer

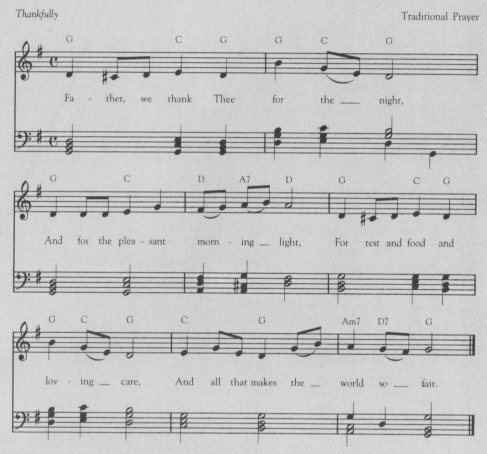

Father, we thank Thee for the ___ night,
And for the plea - sant morn - ing ___ light, For rest and food and
lov - ing ___ care, And all that makes the ___ world so ___ fair.

Help us to do the things we should,
To be to others kind and good,
In all we do, in all we say,
To grow more loving every day.